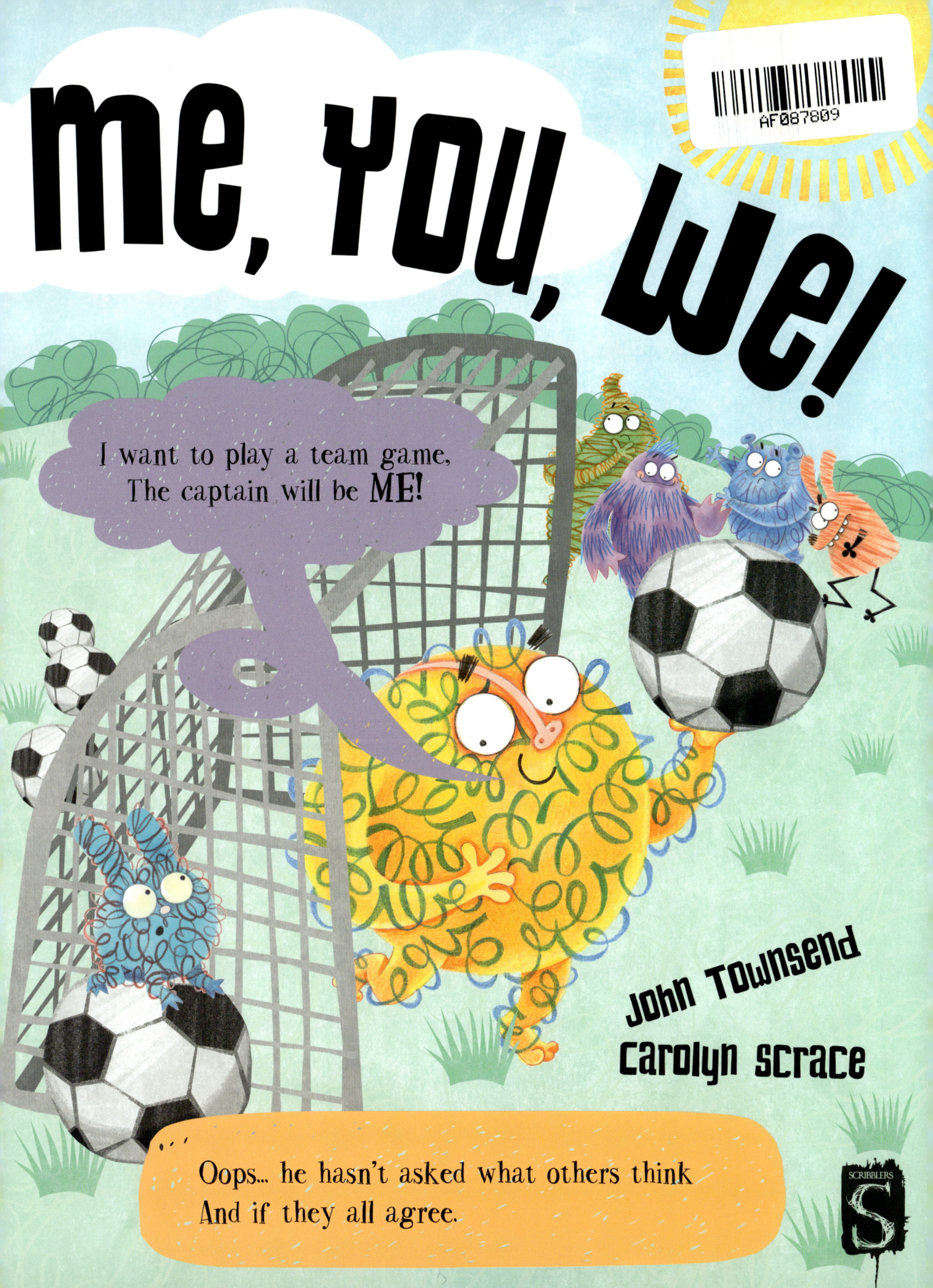

Published in Great Britain in MMXXII by
Scribblers, an imprint of
The Salariya Book Company Ltd
25 Marlborough Place, Brighton BN1 1UB
www.salariya.com

ISBN: 978-1-913971-20-5

SALARIYA
SCRIBO BOOK HOUSE SCRIBBLERS

© The Salariya Book Company Ltd MMXXII

All rights reserved. No part of this publication may be reproduced, stored in or introduced into a retrieval system or transmitted in any form, or by any means (electronic, mechanical, photocopying, recording or otherwise) without the written permission of the publisher. Any person who does any unauthorised act in relation to this publication may be liable to criminal prosecution and civil claims for damages.

1 3 5 7 9 8 6 4 2

A CIP catalogue record for this book is available from the British Library.

This book is sold subject to the conditions that it shall not, by way of trade or otherwise, be lent, resold, hired out, or otherwise circulated without the publisher's prior consent in any form of binding or cover other than that in which it is published and without similar condition being imposed on the subsequent purchaser.

Editor: Nick Pierce

Visit
www.salariya.com
for our online catalogue and
free fun stuff.

PAPER FROM SUSTAINABLE FORESTS

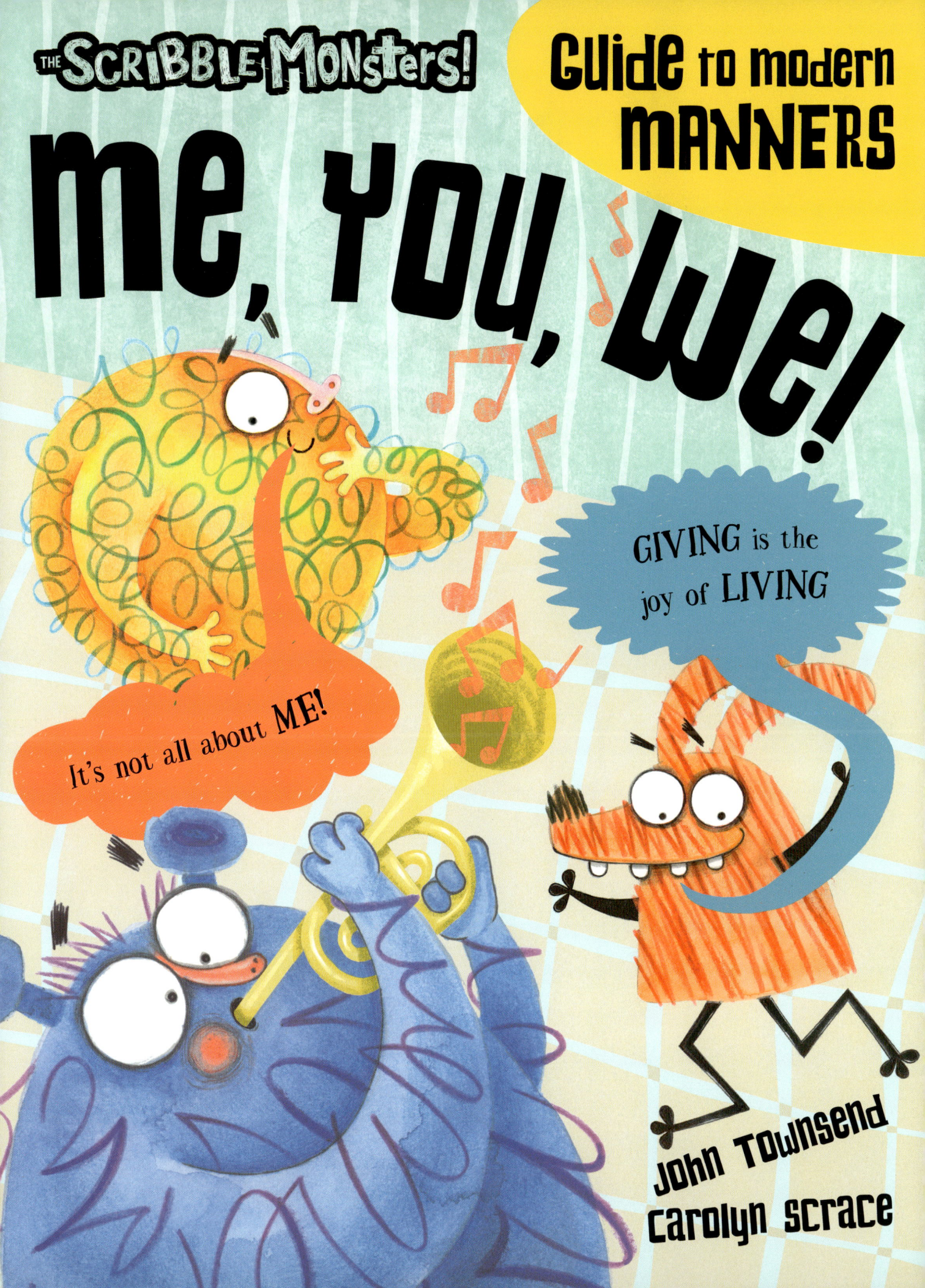

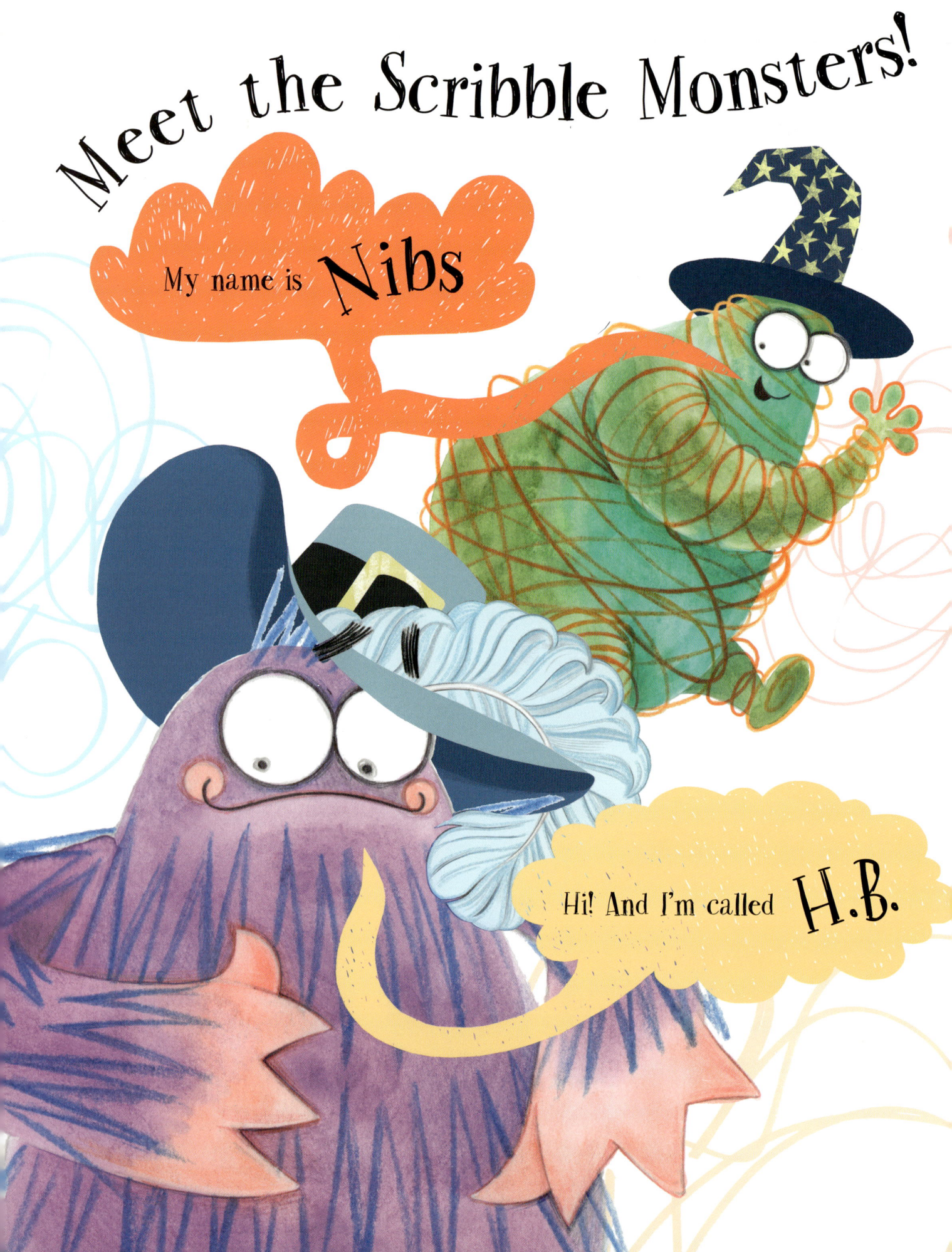

Some little children can forget
To think of others, so...
We're here to scribble our advice
Reminding as we go...

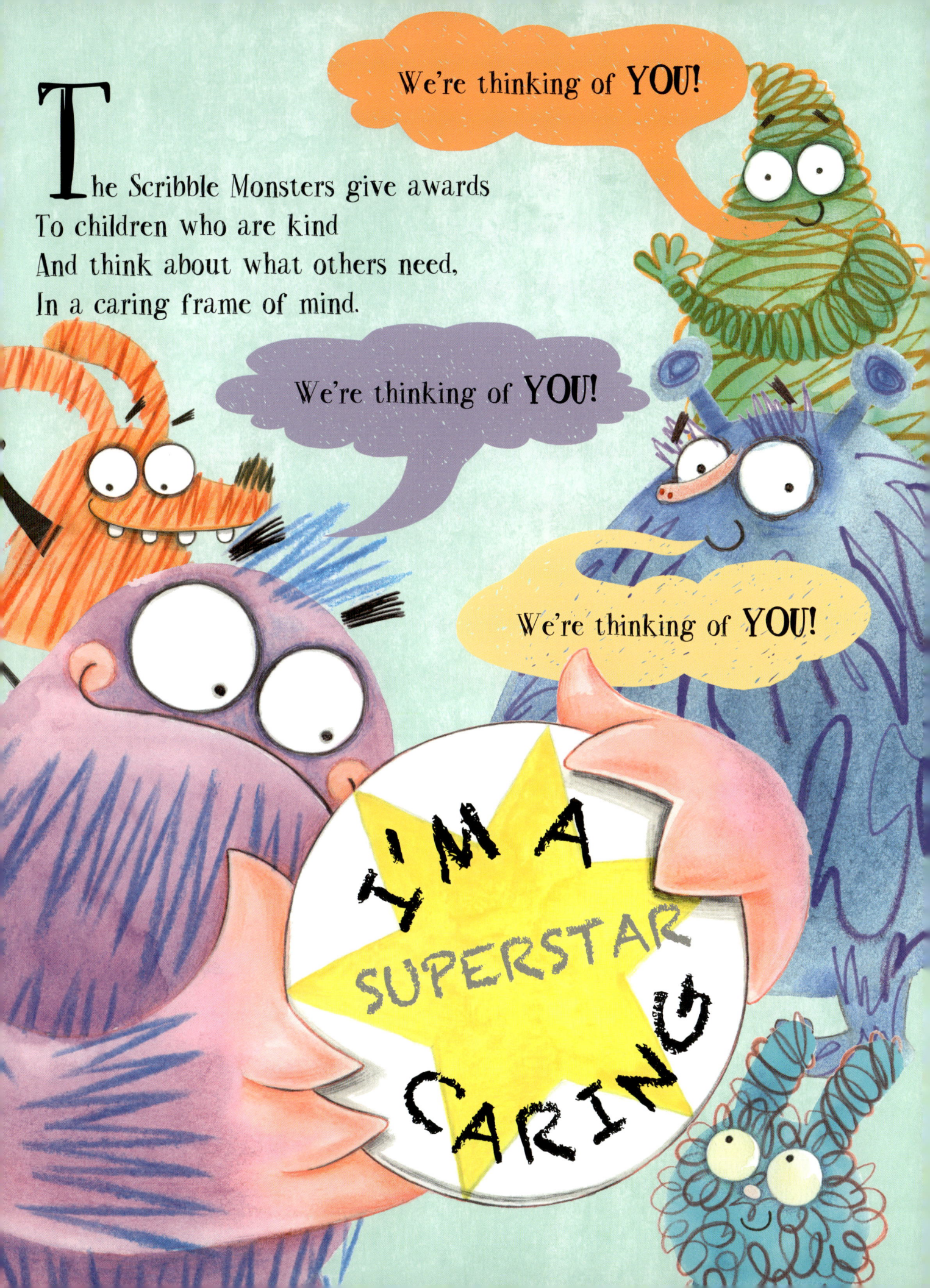

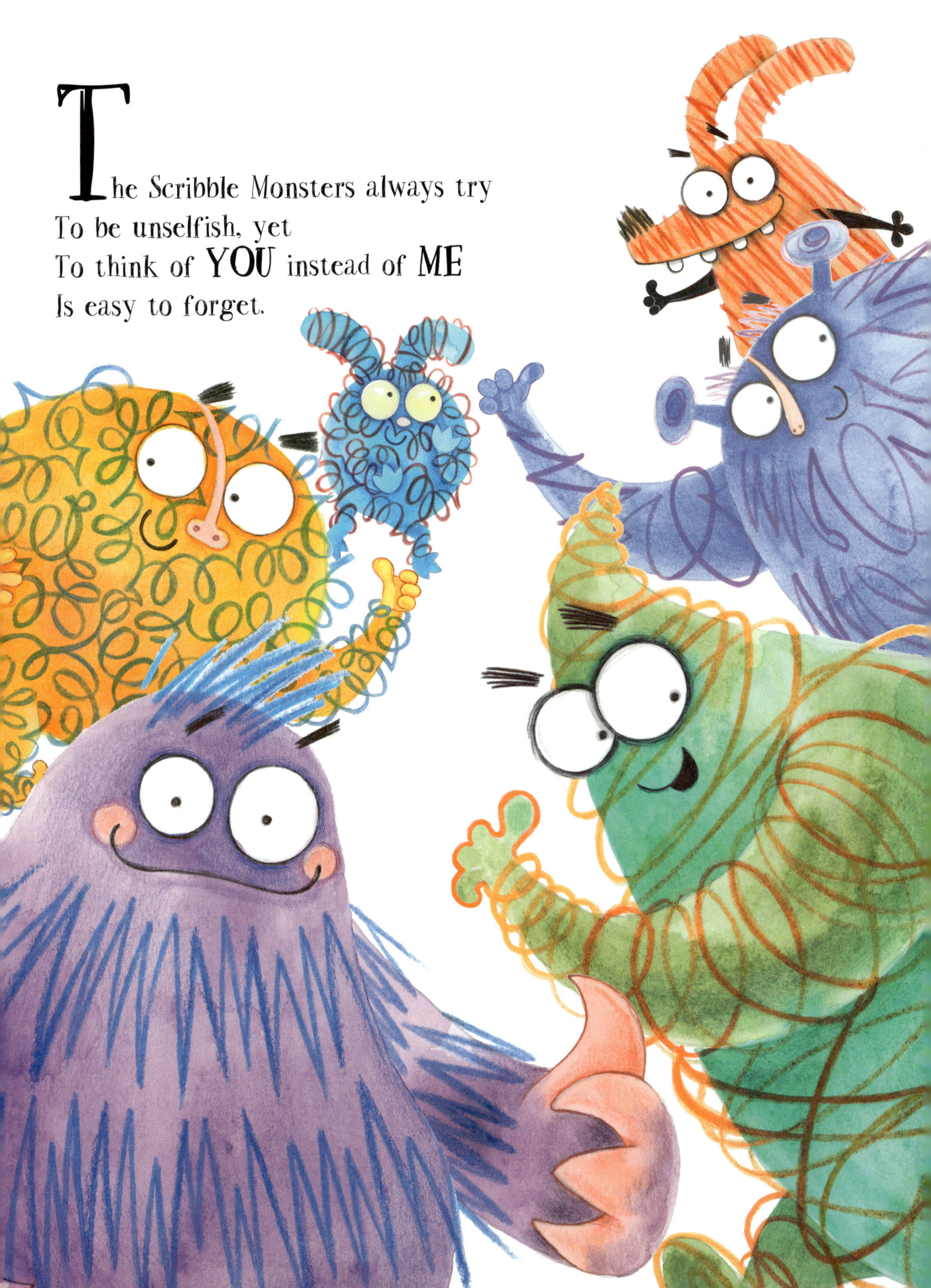

The Scribble Monsters always try
To be unselfish, yet
To think of YOU instead of ME
Is easy to forget.

Pablo wants to play a team game.

The captain will be ME!

Oops... he hasn't asked what others think
And if they all agree.

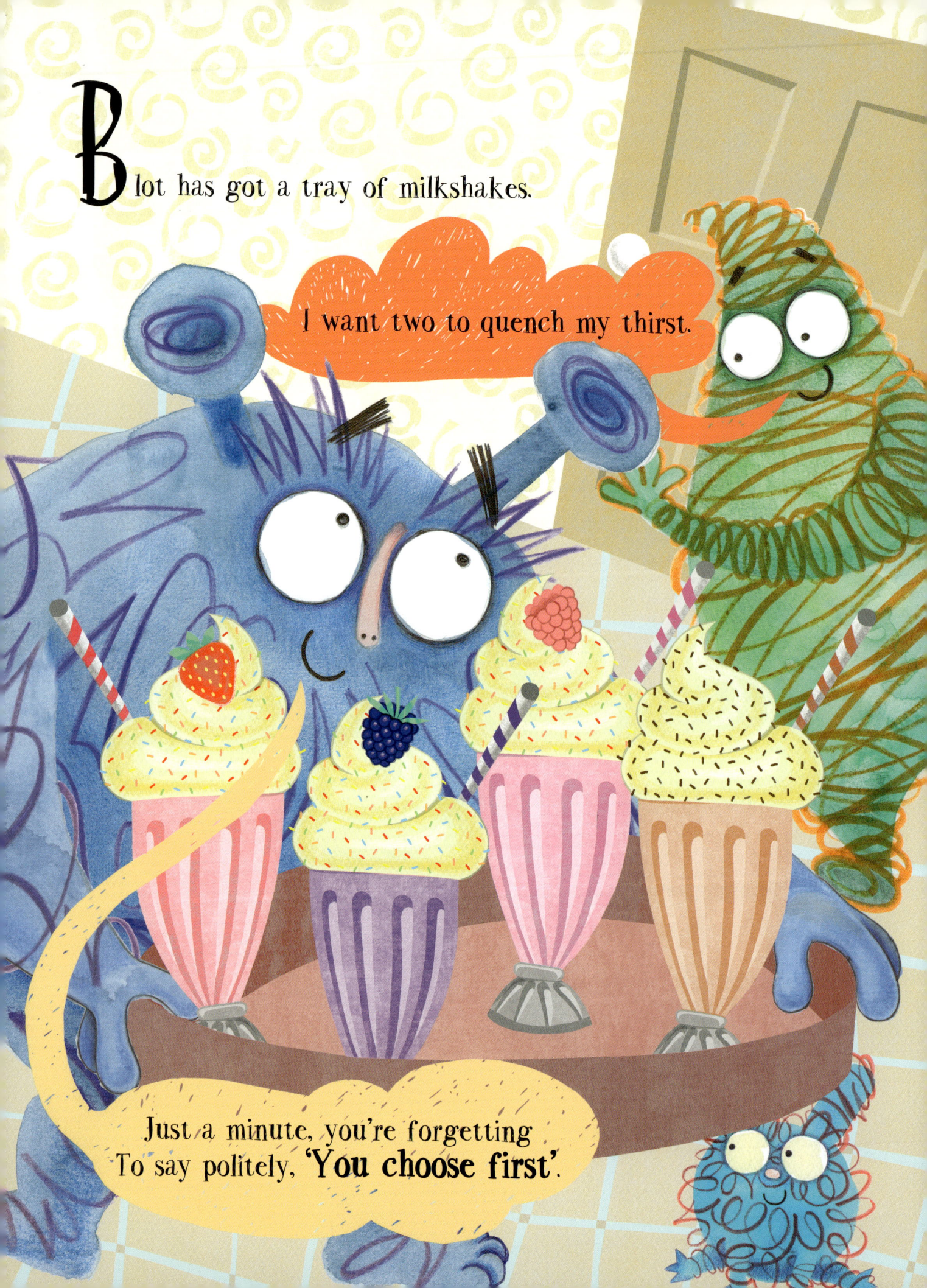

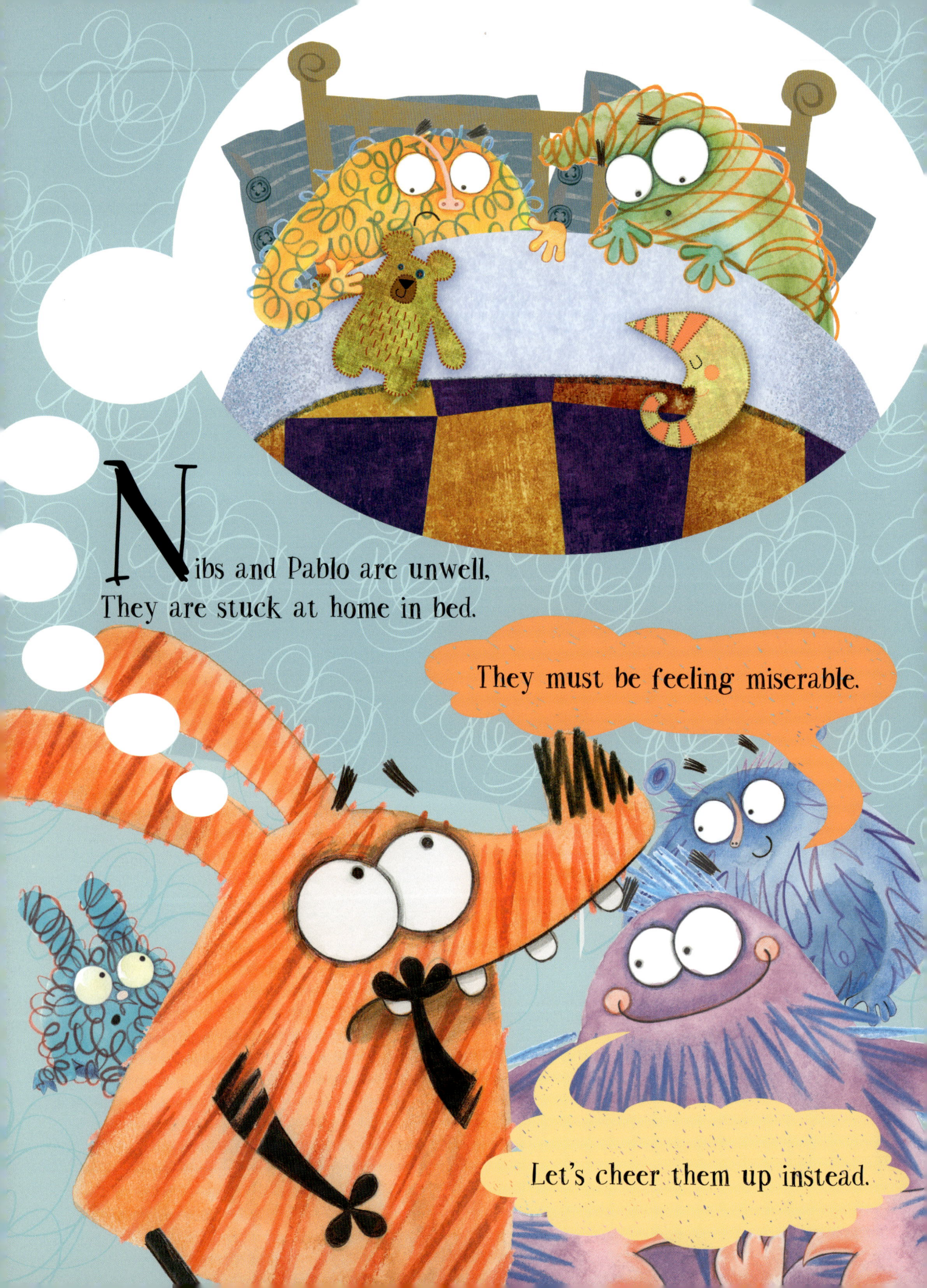

Nibs and Pablo are unwell,
They are stuck at home in bed.

They must be feeling miserable.

Let's cheer them up instead.

Smudge and Inky start to draw
And Blot gets working hard,
While H.B. cuts out sparkly shapes
For each big Get Well card.

Then they sit down at the table.
Everyone knows what to do...
Each plate of food is passed to others
As they giggle, 'AFTER YOU!'

H.B., Inky, Nibs and Pablo,
Blot and Smudge all sing
When they've helped to cheer up others.
They cheer up everything!

HAVE YOU HEARD THE MAGIC WORDS?

GIVING is the joy of LIVING!

The Scribble Monsters wave goodbye
With friendly flags and banners
To help all children to remember
Those **SCRIBBLE MONSTER MANNERS!**

GOOD MANNERS ARE FREE!

I've reversed – now, you first!

QUESTION 3

What makes us all tickled pink?

QUESTION 4

Should I pick which chocolate I want before asking others to choose theirs?

Look at the last page of the book to see if you are right!

GOODBYE!

Goodbye!
Goodbye!
Goodbye!
Goodbye!
Goodbye!

Answers to the quiz:
1. No! I try to think of 'US'.
2. Kind.
3. Children who think of other people.
4. No.
5. After you.
6. No. I should say 'After you'.
7. 'AFTER YOU!'
8. 'ME, YOU, WE!'